"A rich. lyrical story...[with] strikingly beautiful oil pastel illustrations." — *The New York Times Book Review*

Ray is a curious armadillo. and what he is most curious about is the moon. Ray wonders how it can have so many shapes and why it sometimes disappears. He decides to find the answers to his questions by asking his desert animal friends. From the lively. coiling snakes to the prairie dog to the desert grouse. each of Ray's friends has a fanciful explanation of what the moon is. But it isn't until Ray meets up with a wise old owl that he learns exactly how the moon works—and discovers that sometimes the truth is the most unbelievable explanation of all!

John Beifuss's enchanting story is brought to life by Peggy Turley's stunning oil pastel illustrations. Also included is an afterword that gives a brief explanation of the phases of the moon as well as a note about the role that the moon has played in legends around the world. making *Armadillo Ray* a terrific read-aloud story and a vibrant and engaging introduction to astronomy and folklore.

To my parents. Dr. John Paul Beifuss and
Joan Turner Beifuss. —J. B.

To Pamela Brooks Turley. who rescued Ray from my studio floor.
To Betsy and Ginny. the best girls in the world. —P. T.

Text ©1995 by John Beifuss.
Illustrations ©1995 by Peggy Turley.

Book design by Cathleen O'Brien.
Typeset in Greco Adornado and Greco Roman.
The illustrations in this book were rendered in oil pastels.
Manufactured in China.
10   9   8   7   6   5   4

Library of Congress Cataloging-in-Publication Data
Beifuss. John. 1959-
Armadillo Ray / written by John Beifuss:
illustrated by Peggy Turley.   32p. 24.7 x 22.2 cm.
Summary: Curious about the true nature of the moon. Armadillo Ray asks different animals for their opinions.
[1. Armadillos—Fiction.   2. Desert Animals—Fiction.   3. Moon—Fiction.] I. Turley. Peggy. ill. II Title.
PZ7.B38823475Ar   1995   94-44527 [E]—dc20 CIP   AC
ISBN 0-8118-2135-8 (PB)   ISBN 0-8118-0334-1 (HC)

Distributed in Canada by Raincoast Books
9050 Shaughnessy Street. Vancouver. British Columbia V6P 6E5

Chronicle Books LLC
85 Second Street. San Francisco. California 94105
www.chroniclekids.com

ARMADILLO RAY

written by **John Beifuss**

illustrated by **Peggy Turley**

chronicle books · san francisco

Armadillo Ray lived in the desert. where the tumbleweeds rolled past like children turning somersaults.

Like all armadillos. Ray liked to explore at night. When the fierce sun had gone to bed. he would scamper across the cool rocks and dig in the sand with his strong young paws.

When he saw a cactus. he pretended he was a bad guy. "Stick 'em up!" he would say. Ray was an imaginative armadillo.

Ray was also an inquisitive armadillo. Often he would peer into the clear night sky and contemplate the moon.

Some nights the moon was full and round and white, like a blossom on the saguaro cactus where the owls lived. It made the armored shell on Ray's back shine like pebbles in a stream.

Other nights the moon was a half-circle, like the smile of a kit fox reflected sideways in a pool. Or it was only a silver sliver, like the stinger on the tail of a scorpion.

Armadillo Ray was puzzled. What was this magic thing in the sky? How could it have so many shapes? Ray decided to ask the other desert dwellers about the moon.

The first night Ray sought an answer, he came across his friends the snakes. They were dancing. They whipped their snaky bodies into the air.

"Hello!" said Ray.

"Hello!" said the snakes.

"I have a question," said Ray. "What is the moon?"

"What a silly question for a young armadillo!" the snakes said. "Everybody knows the moon is a great serpent that can twist into many different shapes. Some nights it coils into a tight round ball. Tonight. it has bent itself into a shiny crescent. Once the serpent was stretched across the land like a great white belt. but the land began filling up with people. The people crawled across the serpent like the fleas on a coyote. They made the serpent itch. so it crawled up to the sky."

Then the snakes curled and cork-
screwed into hoops and crescents
in imitation of the great serpent.
"I can do that too!" Ray shouted.
And he did.

But Ray was not convinced
the moon was a great white
serpent. He decided to seek
another opinion.

A few nights later, Armadillo Ray traveled deeper into the desert. Soon he came to a prairie dog burrow.

"Hello!" called Ray.

"Hello," answered the prairie dog.

"I have a question," said Ray. "What is the moon?"

"What a silly question for a young armadillo!" the prairie dog said.

"Everybody knows the moon is the entrance to a great burrow in the sky. The father of all prairie dogs lives at the bottom. He sleeps during the day and keeps the light on at night. Sometimes the door to his burrow is open only a crack. He opens it a little more each day. It is half open tonight. In a few nights it will be wide open, a bright white circle of light!"

"The great prairie dog used to live deep in the center of the world, but now there are too many roads. The cars and trucks became so noisy he could not sleep, so he left our world and dug a hole in the sky. If you watch long enough, you can see him poke his head out."

Armadillo Ray and the prairie dog watched the moon move across the sky. But the friends did not see a great prairie dog stick his head out. "There must be too many cars," said the prairie dog.

Ray nodded. Still, he was not convinced that the moon was the entrance to the home of a great prairie dog. He decided to keep searching for an answer.

Several nights later Ray returned to his quest. He soon saw a sage grouse spinning in the brush. She was spreading her wings and ruffling her tail feathers.

"Hello!" said Ray.

"Hello!" said the grouse.

"I have a question." said Ray. "What is the moon?"

"What a silly question for a young armadillo!" said the grouse.

"Everybody knows the moon is a giant egg. The grouse who laid it used the sky as a nest because the desert was too small. And beyond the desert are buildings and steamboats and bridges—things a young armadillo like you wouldn't know about.

"The moon is a magic egg," the grouse continued. "It grows smaller and larger and larger and smaller, over and over and over. But it has never hatched. One day it will crack open and the world's largest grouse will come out. Won't that be the day!"

Before Ray could reply, he heard a noise. It was an owl who lived in a nearby cactus. "Ha!" said the owl. "Don't listen to that grouse. Or the snakes or the prairie dog or the others. I will tell you about the moon."

Ray was happy. "Owls are wise," Ray thought. "He will know what the moon is."

craters

full moon

2160 miles

waning

month

reflection

4.2 billion
years old

76 KM

The owl began to talk. He used
words Ray had never heard
before. On and on he talked. The
night began to slip away.

Armadillo Ray listened and
tried to understand. Fingers of
color scratched the darkness from
the sky. The moon disappeared and
the sun came up.

The owl finished his story. He looked down from the cactus. Ray was lying on the ground, his head on his paws.

Ray knew the owl was wise, and he believed the owl had told him the truth. But somehow the owl's story had seemed the most unbelievable of all. Ray was a tired armadillo.

As Ray closed his eyes in sleep, the moon rose again in his dreams. It seemed to be a great shining armadillo.

WHAT IS THE MOON?

Here is what the owl told Armadillo Ray about the moon.

The moon is the earth's natural satellite. That means that the moon orbits, or travels around, the earth. Unlike the earth, the moon is essentially a dry, dusty rock. It has mountains, and vast plains of hardened lava, and large dents in its surface called craters. To us, these features sometimes look like a face, which is why we say that there is a Man in the Moon. But the moon has no life of any kind—no owls, no snakes, no armadillos, no people.

The moon is very large. If an armadillo could burrow from one side to the other, it would travel about 2160 miles (3476 km). But compared to the earth, the moon is no bigger than a tennis ball next to a basketball. The moon is also very old. It's been around for at least 4.2 billion years.

The moon does not really glow or give off light. Like the earth, its light comes from the sun. At night, people and animals on earth see the sun's light reflecting off the moon. That is why the moon appears to glow. The changes in the moon that so puzzled Armadillo Ray are called phases. It takes about twenty-nine and a half days for the moon to complete its cycle of phases. The moon does not really change shape during these phases. It just looks like it does, because the part of the moon that is lit up by the sun is not always visible from the earth. As the earth and moon move through space, sometimes more of the moon's shadowy side can be seen from the earth, and sometimes more of the light. So the moon on some nights appears to be just a sliver of light, or a crescent, or a half-moon. When all of the sunlit side can be seen from the earth, it is known as a full moon.

MOON LORE

Armadillo Ray and his friends aren't the only ones who have invented stories about the moon. Moon stories have been around for as long as there has been a moon in the sky and creatures with imaginations to look at it from the earth.

An ancient Chinese legend says that the moon is made of water and inhabited by a hare and a toad who like to watch the stars from their home. Some Native American tribes from the Pacific Northwest say the moon was flown into the sky by a mischievous magician in the form of a raven. The Masai people of Africa say the sun and the moon became enemies and got into a brawl. To this day, the legend says, the sun's face is fiery with shame and the moon's face is bruised and battered. These stories show that throughout time, people of all cultures have sought to explain the natural world around them. That is especially true about something as beautiful and mysterious as the moon.

The moon has always been humankind's nighttime companion. In the days before electricity, it was a beacon, warding off the dark. In the days before clocks and calendars, it marked the passage of time. It is no wonder that people have always been fascinated by the ever-changing moon and no wonder that they have imagined magical stories about it. Maybe you have a story of your own.

John Beifuss, a native of Chicago, has been a newspaper reporter in Memphis since 1981. When he was a teenager, his first published article appeared in the late, lamented *Famous Monsters of Filmland* magazine. He is now proud to chronicle the adventures of the world's most existential armadillo. *Armadillo Ray* is his first children's book.

Peggy Turley, amused by her daughters' whimsical animal drawings, created the character Armadillo Ray. He was introduced in a series of narrative paintings exhibited in 1989 and 1990. The images from the 1990 show were the inspiration for this story. Ms. Turley has a B.A. in history from the University of Memphis, where she studied painting and photography. She currently resides in Tennessee.